THIS IGLOO BOOK BELONGS TO:

...........................................

# igloobooks

Published in 2017
by Igloo Books Ltd
Cottage Farm
Sywell
NN6 0BJ
www.igloobooks.com

Original story by Katherine Stano
Illustrated by Scott Brown

Designed by Matthew Ellero
Edited by Caroline Richards

LEO002 0517
2 4 6 8 10 9 7 5 3 1
ISBN 978-1-78670-289-0

Printed and manufactured in China

# Night OWL says Goodnight

igloobooks

Little Night Owl loved to play
with her friends 'til the end of day.
As soon as the sun began to set,
it wasn't Night Owl's bedtime yet.

"There's a special job for you,"
said Wise Owl with a TWIT-T-WOO.
"Help your friends drift off to sleep
by telling stories and counting sheep...

...while other creatures sleep in
bed, night owls stay awake instead."

So Night Owl flew
and flapped up high and
swooped across the evening sky.

Night Owl read to her friends until,
the moon appeared behind the hill.
"Goodnight," she said as she heard them snore,
then tiptoed across the forest floor.

All her friends slept safe at home,
but now Night Owl was all alone.
"There's no one here to play with me.
But wait! What's that up in the tree?"

# "Surprise!"

called her owl friends with a
HOOT and WHOO.
"We're wide-awake, just like you."

"We've all flown over to come and stay.
We've got all night to hoot and play!"

The little owls played all night long,
until they hooted their goodbye song.
Night Owl stretched and started to yawn.
Soon the night would turn into dawn.

"Tonight's been so much fun," she said,
"but now it's time to go to bed."